THE TIME-AGO TALES OF JAHDU

18387

THE TIME-AGO
TALES OF JAHDU

BY VIRGINIA HAMILTON

Illustrated by Nonny Hogrogian

The Macmillan Company

J

For Leigh and Jaime

CONTENTS

How Jahdu Found His Power, 7

How Jahdu Took Care of Trouble, 21

How Young Owl and Almost Everybody
  Grew Tired of Jahdu, 35

How Jahdu Became Himself, 47

HOW JAHDU FOUND HIS POWER

Mama Luka liked to sit in her tight little room in a fine, good place called Harlem. She liked to sit with the window blinds drawn against the sunlight. And Mama Luka did, every day.

Mama Luka had black skin and a nose as curved as the beak of a parrot. She wore her hair in one long pigtail down her back. She called the pigtail her plait, and she could sit on it. She sat on it whenever she felt like telling tales.

Mama Luka took care of Lee Edward after his school was out for the day and until his mother came home from work. And Mama Luka sat all the while in her little room in the good place, telling Jahdu stories to Lee Edward. She told them slow and she told them easy. And Lee Edward listened. He sat on the floor with his eyes tight shut, which was the best way for him to imagine Jahdu.

Lee Edward loved Mama Luka. She sometimes called him Little Brother just like his own mama did. And he loved his own mama, who worked. He loved his papa, too, who worked when he could. Lee Edward loved Jahdu and Jahdu stories. And he loved the way Mama Luka told them like any boy would.

"Now here we go, Little Brother," Mama Luka said one day.

"There are many a-thousand Jahdu stories," she told Lee Edward. "I know about two hundred of them. I've told you a roomful of Jahdu stories. So that leaves one more roomful of Jahdu stories to tell. Now, you pick out of the air in this room one more Jahdu story."

Lee Edward looked around the room. At last he pointed to an empty space just above Mama Luka's head.

"That one," Lee Edward said.

Mama Luka reached above her head. She cupped her hands around the place Lee Edward had pointed out in the air. And she brought her hands down slowly to her face. Mama Luka opened her mouth and swallowed what had been in her hands.

"Lee Edward, you picked a time-ago story out of the air," she said. "It has a strong taste to it, for it tells how Jahdu found out he had magic power."

"So tell it," Lee Edward said to Mama Luka.

"So I'm getting myself ready," said Mama Luka.

"Lee Edward," began Mama Luka, "the story you picked is

about a time not long after Jahdu had been born. He had not much shape then and not much size. And only his face was clear. Jahdu didn't know he had any magic at all.

"Lee Edward, in that time-ago," said Mama Luka, "Jahdu wasn't as tall as you."

"What did his face look like?" asked Lee Edward. He hoped to catch Mama Luka before she had time to think. But Mama Luka wasn't to be caught this day or any other day. No, she wasn't.

"Little Brother, don't you try to trick me," said Mama Luka. "I know better than to talk about the face of Jahdu."

"Just give me a hint," said Lee Edward.

"Child, nobody who has seen the face of Jahdu will tell you what his face looks like. And I have seen it," said Mama Luka, "and I can't tell."

"Well then, get on with the story," said Lee Edward.

"Here it comes," said Mama Luka.

THIS IS THE JAHDU STORY WITH A STRONG TASTE THAT MAMA LUKA TOLD TO LEE EDWARD.

Jahdu was running along. He was two feet tall. Yes, he was. And he had been in the world one year.

Jahdu lived high atop the Mountain of Paths. He made his home in the only black gum tupelo tree in the pine forest covering the mountain. From his tree, Jahdu could see all the paths to the valley below. He could see which paths the animal children who lived on the mountain walked along.

Jahdu believed the paths the animal children walked along were good and safe. And only these good and safe paths would Jahdu run along.

But Jahdu was only a year in the world. He did not yet know everything. No, he didn't. One day Jahdu was running along a path behind some animal children. All at once the animal children stopped still.

A bandicoot rat fell to the ground. He grew stiff and he screamed and cried loudly for his mother.

A brown bear cub stood up on one hind leg. He hopped in circles, bumping into a fawn and stepping on a baby otter. The brown bear cub sang a wordless song. The young woodchuck, the raccoon girl and the wolf child wandered away into the pine wood and were lost. Some of the other animal children sat down on the path, moaning to themselves and trembling all over.

It took Jahdu an hour to gather all of the animal children on the path again. Then he tied a rope around all of them and led them to another path he knew to be good and safe. There, he let them loose.

"I'd better go back to that first path," Jahdu said. "I'd better find out as fast as I can what caused those animal children to stop still and hop around and fall down and act silly."

Jahdu found the path on which the animal children had stopped still. As he went running down the path, something he couldn't see tried to catch him. But Jahdu was stronger than whatever it was that tried to stop him. He kept right on running along.

"Woogily!" whispered Jahdu to himself. "There are baneberries

12

growing on both sides of this path. Everybody knows baneberries can make animal children sick. I'd better keep on this path to find out what it is that tries to catch me. I'd better find out why baneberries grow on both sides of a good and safe path."

Jahdu stayed on the path. Yes, he did. All at once Jahdu fell into a hole full of thorns.

"Ouch!" said Jahdu. "Thorns have points to hurt Jahdu!" Jahdu jumped out of the hole and bounced into a soft bed of sweet-smelling leaves.

"Woogily!" said Jahdu. "This funny path has good and bad about it. But it surely isn't safe for animal children to walk along."

Jahdu kept right on the good and bad path with baneberries on both sides of it, full of thorn holes and soft beds of sweet-smelling leaves. He ran and he ran until he came to a stream. He sat down in the middle of the stream to cool himself. Suddenly thirteen crawfish started pinching Jahdu. He leaped out of the water.

"Woogily!" said Jahdu. "That's a nice little stream so fresh and cold. But it has thirteen crawfish that can pinch the paws of little animals. I'd better hurry and find out where this funny path ends."

So Jahdu kept on hurrying along the good and bad path with baneberries on both sides, with thorn holes and soft beds of sweet-smelling leaves, and a stream across it with thirteen crawfish.

All at once Jahdu ran smack into a banyan tree at the end of the path. He bounced clear around the banyan tree. Yes, he did. He started running again and ran smack into the banyan tree once more.

"Woogily!" cried Jahdu. "How in the world did a banyan tree get into these pine woods on the Mountain of Paths? Running into banyan trees doesn't feel very good. Little animals will hurt themselves if they go walking into banyan trees!"

Up in the banyan tree was an animal who had a round, sweet face and a bell on its head. And up in the banyan tree was another animal who had a square, mean face and no bell anywhere. Both animals lay side by side peering down at Jahdu.

"I've never seen animals such as you," said Jahdu. "What in the world are you called?"

The animal with a bell on its head spoke first to Jahdu. "I'm called Sweetdream," it said in a soft, sweet voice.

"And I'm Nightmare," said the other animal in a harsh, mean voice. "You're Jahdu and we don't like you."

"Oh, for goodness sake!" said Jahdu. "Like me or not, I'm here to stay. And please tell me why there's a banyan tree at the end of a path on which little animals might walk."

"Because it's here," said Nightmare in a mean voice, "just as Sweetdream and I are here and the path is here, so there!"

"When the bell on my head tinkles," said Sweetdream, "Nightmare and I know little animals are walking along our path."

"Then we use our charms to get them," said Nightmare. "It's such fun watching our spells work on them."

"Just how do your spells work on the little animals?" asked Jahdu.

"Well," said Sweetdream, "my spell makes the animals stop still, then hop around and sing sweet songs, and do and say whatever sweet things are in their heads when my spell strikes them."

"And my spell makes them grow stiff," said Nightmare. "They fall to the ground and scream and cry. Or they moan and tremble all over and do whatever bad things are in their thoughts when my spell strikes them."

"Little animals ought to be able to walk along and do as they wish," said Jahdu. "I don't think it's right to use spells on them."

"I don't care what you think," said Sweetdream sweetly. "I do as I please."

"There's nothing you can do to stop *me*," said Nightmare, "so you better go on your way."

Jahdu was angry. He ran to the banyan tree and shook it as hard as he could.

"Come down from that banyan tree, you awful things!" Jahdu yelled. "Come down and I'll surely take care of you!"

16

Jahdu shook and shook the banyan tree until both animals sitting in it turned purple all over.

"Stop it!" said Sweetdream and Nightmare. "You're making us dizzy and sick!"

"Then come down," said Jahdu, "so Jahdu can take care of you."

"We can't come down," said Sweetdream. "We're attached to this banyan, we can't ever come down!"

Then Jahdu saw that the two animals were growing like figs on the banyan's branches.

"Woogily!" he said. "Now Jahdu's caught you for sure!"

Jahdu ran around and around the banyan tree as fast as he could. He was showing off for the two tree-grown animals. Yes, he was. And he ran so fast he shook the dust right out of himself.

Jahdu's dust rose up into the banyan tree. It settled on Sweetdream and Nightmare and they fell fast asleep.

Jahdu stopped running.

"Woogily!" he said. "Did I do that? Did my dust put Sweetdream and Nightmare to sleep?"

Wherever the Jahdu dust fell, it put things to sleep. A spider walking along the banyan tree trunk got Jahdu dust on him and fell asleep. A bluebird flying low near the banyan tree got a whiff of the Jahdu dust and had to land in the tree. As the Jahdu dust settled on the bluebird, it fell asleep.

"Woogily!" said Jahdu. "I've got me some magic! I can put things to sleep! Maybe I have more magic. Let me see."

Jahdu tried wishing there was no good and bad path, no Sweetdream and Nightmare and no banyan tree. But this didn't work. No, it didn't. For the path stayed. So did the banyan tree and the sleeping Sweetdream and Nightmare.

Jahdu had another idea. He started running around the banyan tree. Jahdu ran slower and slower and ever so slowly.

The Jahdu dust rose off the two animals up the banyan tree. It rose off the tree trunk and the spider, off the bluebird and off everything. Then the Jahdu dust fell back into Jahdu. All that had been asleep woke up. Sweetdream and Nightmare yawned and stared down at Jahdu.

"Woogily!" said Jahdu. "I can wake things up. I've got me another magic!"

"You shouldn't have put us to sleep," said Sweetdream. "We have to work in the daytime so we can watch the fun."

"You won't watch the fun anymore," said Jahdu, "for I'm going to make you work at night."

"You can't make us do anything we don't want to do," said Nightmare.

"If you don't do what I want you to do, I'll put you to sleep for a week," Jahdu told Nightmare.

"Oh, no," said Sweetdream. "Please don't put him to sleep for a week."

"A month," said Jahdu, feeling good all over.

"All right, you have us," said Nightmare. "Just don't get carried away."

Jahdu drew himself up two feet tall. Yes, he did. And he told

Sweetdream and Nightmare what he was going to make them do.

"Nightmare will sleep from daylight to nightfall," said Jahdu. "He will work his spell only at night and only on sleeping animals. And if I ever catch him playing around with his spell when it's daylight, I'll put him to sleep for a year!"

Nightmare looked glum but he didn't say a word. He still felt sick from Jahdu's shaking the banyan tree.

"As for Sweetdream," said Jahdu, "she'll work her spell in the daytime only on those little animals who sleep by day. And then only once in a very long while. The rest of her work she will do at night and on sleeping animals, just the same as Nightmare."

Sweetdream smiled sweetly but said nothing.

"I'll never have any fun again watching my spell work," muttered Nightmare.

"That's the truth," said Jahdu. "I'm getting rid of that awful path, too. I'll put it to sleep for the rest of time!"

And so Jahdu did. He ran up and down the path as fast as he could go. Jahdu dust rose from Jahdu and fell all over the path. At once the path was fast asleep. The baneberries on both sides of the path dried up and slept, too. All kinds of forest plants started growing over the path.

Jahdu stood where once the path had begun. Now, young pine saplings started growing there. Jahdu shouted down the path at Sweetdream and Nightmare.

"Your path is gone," Jahdu shouted. "No little animals will come along here! Now you'll have to send your charms out on the night air. Your spells will never again be very strong. For the night air is so light it can carry only a little of your charms at a time!"

Jahdu went running along. Yes, he did. He could run very fast and he could run very slow. He could shake Jahdu dust out of himself and cause it to fall back into himself again. With his magic he could wake things up and put things to sleep.

THIS IS THE END OF THE JAHDU STORY WITH A STRONG TASTE THAT MAMA LUKA TOLD TO LEE EDWARD.

HOW JAHDU TOOK CARE OF TROUBLE

Mama Luka liked to eat red licorice candy better than any other kind of candy. One day she sat in her room with a jar of red licorice beside her.

Mama Luka held out a red licorice twist to Lee Edward, who sat on the floor. She took a piece for herself and ate it slowly. Then Mama Luka sat on her plait and looked at Lee Edward.

Lee Edward pointed to a space in the air about a foot in front of him. Mama Luka reached for the space. She almost dropped the space before she finally got it on her lap.

Mama Luka said, "You picked a heavy Jahdu story out of the air this time, you surely did, Lee Edward."

Mama Luka patted and shaped whatever it was in her lap that

Lee Edward couldn't see. "I don't think I'll taste this one," Mama Luka said, "for I know it can't taste good."

"Why is this Jahdu story a heavy one," asked Lee Edward, "and why won't it taste good?"

"Well, because, child," Mama Luka said, "after what happened to Jahdu in this story, Jahdu was different."

"How was he different?" asked Lee Edward.

Mama Luka smiled to herself and patted whatever it was in her lap that Lee Edward couldn't see. "Little Brother, I sure wish you hadn't picked this story out of the air," she said.

"Well, tell it so I can know how Jahdu was different," said Lee Edward.

"I'm getting myself ready," said Mama Luka.

THIS IS THE HEAVY JAHDU STORY THAT MAMA LUKA TOLD ONE DAY TO THE CHILD, LEE EDWARD.

Jahdu was running along. He had been running all over for many a year. Now Jahdu was hurrying southward through an empty land. And he whispered to himself as he ran.

"Woogily!" whispered Jahdu. "This empty land takes Jahdu too long to run through. I've seen a few trees but I haven't seen anything else."

Just then, a strong wind blew in Jahdu's face. Jahdu heard a swishing sound. Coming out of the south he saw thirty-two members of a tumbleweed family. They were heading north and they passed Jahdu in a hurry.

"Hey, there!" Jahdu called after the tumbleweeds. "What's the big hurry? Wait up a minute." Jahdu started running northward. But the wind helped the tumbleweeds more than it did him. Jahdu soon found there was no catching those thirty-two tumbleweeds.

"Jahdu, you're a long way from home," one tumbleweed shouted back.

"I like to be always running along," Jahdu told him. "But what's your hurry?"

"We're the last to leave here," the tumbleweed shouted. "We want to reach the mountains in the north before nightfall."

"You were lucky to catch such a swift wind," called Jahdu. "If you'll wait just a minute, I'll go along with you. I'm pretty much tired of this long, empty land."

"We can't wait for you," all the tumbleweeds called. "But do follow us north, Jahdu, for southward lies trouble."

"Trouble?" said Jahdu. He stopped running. "Hey, tumble-weeds," shouted Jahdu. "What is it you said?"

The tumbleweeds called from far away. "Follow us, Jahdu, for southward lies trouble . . . lies trouble . . ." And the tumbleweeds were gone to the north.

"Woogily!" said Jahdu. "Those tumbleweeds surely were in a hurry. I wonder what kind of thing is trouble. I'd better go south-ward and see."

So Jahdu went hurrying on. He ran and he ran southward through the long, empty land. He saw a few tall trees but not one sound did he hear.

"Woogily!" Jahdu said. "There are mountains to southward. Those thirty-two tumbleweeds need not have gone north. Jahdu likes mountains much better than empty land."

Jahdu ran more softly as he came closer to the mountains. The mountains were not like any he had known. When Jahdu was quite close, the mountains moved. Yes, they did.

The mountains sat up with a great creaking sound. Then they stared hard at Jahdu.

"Woogily!" said Jahdu, coming to a stop. "What in the world kind of sitting mountains are *you*!"

The mountains shook all over. They made a noise like thunder that made Jahdu tremble. "I'm no mountains, friend. I'm the giant, Trouble. Come up closer, friend, so Trouble can see what you're made of."

"Oh, no, thank you," said Jahdu. "I'm really just passing through. I've known all kinds of mountains and a number of tumbleweeds," added Jahdu, "but I've never known anything called the giant, Trouble."

"Well, now you do," said Trouble in a voice like drums. "And what might you be called, little friend?"

"You mean to say you've never heard of Jahdu?" asked Jahdu.

"Never in my life," said the giant, Trouble.

"Everyone knows me," said Jahdu. "I am Jahdu who is always running along. I'm three feet tall. I live in a tupelo tree when I'm at home. And I have magic which I keep to myself."

Trouble laughed loudly. "You come too close to Trouble, Jahdu," said the giant. "I think I'll just keep you from running along."

The great right hand of Trouble swooped down. Yes, it did. But Jahdu had already started running away. Jahdu ran and he ran. The great right hand of Trouble just missed him.

The great left hand of Trouble swooped down. Jahdu managed to slip through its fingers. Trouble laughed in a thunderous roar. He stretched himself out along the southward landscape and propped himself up on his elbow.

Jahdu stayed out of the reach of Trouble without letting Trouble out of his sight. He could see that Trouble was no kind of mountain. For Trouble was bigger than fifty-two mountains.

The giant, Trouble, was clothed in gray. His eyes were rain-cloud dark and his face had about it the anger of a storm.

"Trouble's teeth flash like lightning," thought Jahdu. "And what a large earring he wears on his right ear."

"What are you staring at, Jahdu?" the giant, Trouble, asked. "You like my ears? Oh, it's my earring you stare at. Come closer, Jahdu, and I'll show it to you."

"Oh, no, thank you," said Jahdu. "I really have to be running on."

But Jahdu kept right on staring at the giant, Trouble. Trouble's feet were as big as steamships. His legs were as long as highways.

Attached to Trouble's ear was a gold loop as round and bright as the moon. An upright blue keg hung from the gold loop. The keg was as large as a water tower and screams and cries came from inside it.

"What in the world are those sounds from your earring?" asked Jahdu.

"Why, Jahdu, old friend, that's Trouble's barrel," said the giant. "I love all my friends, so I keep them with me!" Then Trouble laughed like thunder.

"Well, the friends you love are screaming," said Jahdu to the giant. "I'm sure they want you to let them out."

"Screams and cries are sounds I like best," said the giant. "Besides, no one I put in my barrel has ever got out again."

"But what sort of friends would even a giant like you treat so badly?" asked Jahdu.

"All kinds of friends," Trouble said. "I don't care if they are good or bad or big or little. Trouble treats every kind of folks just the same. I never bother them but they seek me out and swarm over me like flies."

"Woogily!" said Jahdu. "I surely wouldn't want to end up like a fly in your barrel!"

"Oh, come, come!" said Trouble. "Take a look. I've got a whole bunch of fine folks traveling with me."

With one huge finger, Trouble tipped his barrel so Jahdu could see inside. Staying out of Trouble's reach, Jahdu climbed the tallest tree he could find to have a look.

"That's about the worst sight I've ever seen," said Jahdu.

Jahdu saw all manner of flying birds in the barrel. He saw forest animals. He saw a lion. He saw mothers and fathers and babies and donkeys. He saw all kinds of life in that awful barrel of Trouble.

Now Jahdu grew angry. His face looked fierce. He knew he didn't like the giant, Trouble, at all. Suddenly Jahdu thought of a plan to free all those who were in Trouble's barrel.

Jahdu climbed down the tree and started running along close to the giant.

"You must set them loose," Jahdu said to Trouble. "If you don't put that barrel down on the ground and let everybody out, I will have to free them myself!"

"Come ahead, little Jahdu," said the giant. "Come right on in." When Jahdu came close to the giant, Trouble's hand swooped down in a rush of wind and scooped him up.

"Oh, please, giant, Trouble, don't put me in your barrel," said Jahdu. "I was really just running along." He pretended to be frightened and moaned as loudly as he could.

"You won't run along ever again," said Trouble. And, plop! He dropped Jahdu into his barrel.

"It's Jahdu!" shouted everybody in the barrel. "Trouble's caught Jahdu! It's the end of us for sure!"

"Hi, everybody!" said Jahdu. "I want all of you to gather around close to me, please. We're getting out of here!"

"We are?" everybody asked.

"Of course," said Jahdu. "Do you think I would have allowed Trouble to catch me if I wasn't planning to get free again?"

"Oh, Jahdu, you're wonderful!" everybody said.

Jahdu felt so good he said, "Woogily!" in a loud voice. Then Jahdu told everybody what they must do.

"Mothers and fathers, dig under the walls of this barrel. Babies, you scratch at the sides. Birds, you peck away. Donkeys, you kick. You, lion, use your claws to tear at the floors. We've got to make lots of holes. Now, cows and horses, set up a mooing and neighing so Trouble won't know what's going on."

Everybody did what Jahdu said to do. After an hour not one of them had made a dent in Trouble's barrel.

"Woogily!" whispered Jahdu. "It will take forever to get us out of *this* barrel of Trouble. I see I'm going to have to outsmart that giant if I'm to free his friends."

While everybody was busy digging and neighing and scratching and clawing, Jahdu started running around the barrel. He ran faster and faster. Yes, he did. Soon the dust of himself rose up in the barrel. The Jahdu dust settled on everybody. And one by one, everybody in the barrel fell fast asleep. When every-

body was asleep, Jahdu lay down and pretended he was asleep also.

Now Trouble still lay across the southward landscape listening to the screams and cries from his barrel. The screams and cries were like music to his ears. But after a time, Trouble didn't hear even one scream or cry.

"Hey, friends," Trouble called out of the side of his mouth. "Sing a little louder. I can't hear you."

Not one sound came from Trouble's barrel. Trouble took off his earring and peered inside the barrel. He couldn't believe his eyes. No, he couldn't. For he found everybody stretched out at the bottom of the barrel.

"Why, they've all fainted from the heat. Even the last one's fainted—little Jahdu," said the giant.

Carefully Trouble gathered everybody and Jahdu from the bottom of the barrel. And he laid everybody and Jahdu out on the ground.

"They need to lie down by a cool mountain lake for awhile," Trouble said. "Let's see. There's a lake in the mountains northward. I'll lay them over there."

Trouble picked up everybody and Jahdu in one hand. He stood up and held out his arm across the long, empty land to the mountains in the north. Then Trouble set everybody and Jahdu down beside a cool mountain lake.

Said the giant, "I'll give my friends a chance to cool themselves now so they will feel more like screaming and crying later."

Again, Trouble lay down across the southward landscape. At once Jahdu got up and began running along. He ran as slowly as he knew how. Soon Jahdu dust rose off everybody and settled back into Jahdu. Everybody woke up. Yes, they did.

"We are in the mountains in the north," Jahdu told everybody. "I've outsmarted Trouble," added Jahdu. "He still lies resting, so be quiet and hear what I say."

"Those who live in water, dive deep under water and stay hidden as long as you can. Those who like holes, go hide in holes. Everybody else, follow the lion, for he knows where to find the oldest mountain cave. Trouble is sure to come searching for all of us soon, so hurry!"

It was not long before Trouble stood up and looked across the long, empty land for his friends beside the mountain lake. He saw only Jahdu, who was running along just out of the reach of Trouble's long arm.

"Little Jahdu," Trouble said, "that's the first time anybody has ever tricked me."

"I didn't trick you at all," said Jahdu. "I used my head and my magic. I thought of a plan to outsmart you. There's no need for you to search for your friends either," Jahdu added. "You might find two or three of them but you'll never find everybody."

The giant shook with laughter, making the earth tremble. "I don't need to go looking for them, little friend," he said to Jahdu. "I've never had to go looking for anybody. For it's the truth that everybody comes looking for Trouble and they always will."

"Not *me!*" said Jahdu. "I'll not come looking for you ever again!"

"Oh, sure you will," said Trouble. "You won't be able to help yourself. So, good-bye, little friend, until the next time." Trouble turned away. With three of his giant steps he was out of sight beyond the long, empty land.

"Woogily!" whispered Jahdu. "I hope I never run into Trouble again!"

So it was that Jahdu met Trouble and was able to outsmart him. And Jahdu came to believe he was smarter than anyone.

THIS IS THE END OF THE HEAVY JAHDU STORY MAMA LUKA TOLD ONE DAY TO THE CHILD, LEE EDWARD.

HOW YOUNG OWL AND ALMOST EVERYBODY GREW TIRED OF JAHDU

Mama Luka sat quietly in her tight little room. She hummed a tune to herself as she waited for Lee Edward to get settled on the floor. She did not sit on her plait this day. For Mama Luka had just finished combing her hair and now she braided it all the way down to her knees.

Lee Edward sat still. He watched Mama Luka as he always did. He waited without saying a word until Mama Luka had finished braiding her hair.

"Well, child," Mama Luka said at last. "I've been telling you Jahdu stories for many an afternoon."

"Yes," said Lee Edward.

"Pretty soon it will be summer," said Mama Luka. "Come summer, your mama will have you stay with me most of the day."

"I know," said Lee Edward, smiling. "And then you'll have time to tell me more than one Jahdu story a day."

Mama Luka nodded and folded her round, soft hands in her lap. "Little Brother, do you like the Jahdu stories?" she asked.

"I love them," said Lee Edward. "I love Jahdu, too." Then Lee Edward grew shy with Mama Luka. "I love you, too, Mama Luka," he said, softly.

"You're a fine boy, Lee Edward," said Mama Luka. "Not like some boys I've told the Jahdu stories to. I just want to be sure you will always love Jahdu."

"I always will," said Lee Edward.

"I told you once that Jahdu was different after he met up with the giant, Trouble," said Mama Luka.

"I remember that," Lee Edward said, "but I haven't been able to pick a story out of the air that shows how he was different. He's always Jahdu helping everyone."

"That's why today I will pick out of the air a simple little Jahdu story," Mama Luka told Lee Edward. "It will clearly show you how full of mischief Jahdu could be sometimes."

"How was he full of mischief?" asked Lee Edward.

"Jahdu tried to outsmart everybody," Mama Luka said.

"But why did he try to do that?" Lee Edward wanted to know.

Mama Luka smiled. "Child," she said, "Jahdu had outwitted a giant bigger than fifty-two mountains and nobody had ever done that. So Jahdu *had* to think he was smarter than everybody else."

"It wasn't right for Jahdu to outwit everybody just because he was smarter," Lee Edward said.

"I know that and you know that," Mama Luka said, "but Jahdu didn't know that. How was he to know outsmarting anybody could be wrong?"

"It had been right for him to outsmart Trouble," Lee Edward said.

"And that's the truth," said Mama Luka.

"I'm glad Jahdu wasn't bad," Lee Edward said.

"Little Brother, so am I!" said Mama Luka.

All at once Mama Luka bent forward. Something Lee Edward couldn't see passed by Mama Luka. With her eyes Mama Luka followed what Lee Edward couldn't see. When whatever it was passed over her left shoulder, she grabbed it. Mama Luka brought whatever it was up to her mouth and swallowed it. She leaned back in her chair and looked at Lee Edward.

"Yes, child," she said. "The story I just picked out of the air surely is the one that shows best how Jahdu played tricks on everybody."

"I want to hear the story," said Lee Edward.

"I'm getting myself ready," said Mama Luka.

THIS IS THE JAHDU STORY FILLED WITH MISCHIEF THAT MAMA LUKA TOLD TO LEE EDWARD.

Jahdu was running along. He had been running along over most of the world. Sometimes he stopped awhile. But he never stayed very long in any one place. For wherever he stopped, he outsmarted anybody he came across. Anybody who had once been tricked by Jahdu would never let Jahdu get close enough to outwit him again.

One fine day Jahdu was running in a new place. The place was a wood with tall trees close together. The wood was warm and wet and in it vines grew thick and round as big snakes. Sometimes Jahdu liked swinging along on the vines when the ground was too wet for him to run along.

Jahdu carried a pink cage shaped like a bell with six parakeets in it. He had tied the cage to himself with a piece of rope he had found. Jahdu had taken the cage from a man who sold them. He had grabbed the cage from the man without paying for it or for the parakeets in it. When the man shouted for Jahdu to bring the cage and the birds back, Jahdu opened the cage and all of the parakeets flew away. The man had been angry at Jahdu. But Jahdu had kept on running. He had laughed and laughed about taking the cage and letting the parakeets out.

Jahdu was running through the wood in this warm and damp new place. Besides the parakeet cage tied to him, Jahdu carried a can of blue paint on his head. There was a small black brush sticking out of the paint.

Jahdu had taken the blue paint from a farmer's wife who had been painting a gray kitchen chair blue. He took the paint when she wasn't looking. In its place Jahdu put a small can of white paint. He had taken the white paint from a house painter he had found painting the window sills of a house.

Jahdu stayed around long enough to watch the farmer's wife pick up the brush in the white paint. The farmer's wife started painting her chair. When she saw it turning white before her eyes, she screamed and jumped away.

Jahdu laughed and laughed at the farmer's wife. Yes, he did. Then he went right on running along through the wood in a new place, with the parakeet cage tied to him and the can of blue paint balanced on his head.

The ground became too wet, so Jahdu grabbed a vine and was swinging along, when suddenly he heard a sound of moaning and groaning.

"Ohhhh. Hooooo," the sound went.

"Woogily!" said Jahdu. "What in the world kind of sound is that?"

Jahdu stopped his swinging along. Yes, he did. He sat in a tree and listened.

"Ohhhh. Hooooo," the sound went again.

The moaning and groaning sound came from the tree across from the one in which Jahdu sat. Then Jahdu saw a hollow high up in the trunk of the tree opposite him.

"That is the worst moaning and groaning sound I've heard in a long time," said Jahdu. "I bet that an owl has made his nest in that hole up there. Owls are the worst moaners and groaners in the world. I think I'll stop awhile and have me some fun."

Jahdu hung his parakeet cage from a branch of the tree he was sitting in. He climbed down the tree and placed the can of blue paint on the ground behind the tree. Then he crossed over to the tree where he had seen the hollow in the high branches.

"Hey, there," Jahdu called. "Who is it I hear up there moaning and groaning worse than anyone?"

For a moment there was silence high up in the tree. But soon the moaning and groaning began again.

"I'd better climb up there," Jahdu whispered. He climbed up the tree and peered into the hollow. Jahdu found a small screech owl leaning sadly against the wall of his nest. The owl moaned and groaned and held the feather tufts on his head.

"What in the world is the matter with you?" asked Jahdu.

The owl opened his eyes wide and rolled them from side to side. "It's raining, isn't it?" said the owl. "It's pouring rain, isn't it? It's been pouring down rain for days, hasn't it? I knew it! Now the headache I've had for two days won't ever go away!"

"Oh, for goodness sake," said Jahdu. "It's not raining at all. The sun is blazing in a sky as blue as can be. There isn't a cloud for miles."

"Who are you?" asked the screech owl, blinking at Jahdu.

Jahdu thought quickly. He didn't want to tell the owl he was Jahdu. No, he didn't. For if the owl had heard of Jahdu he would surely fly away.

"I'm a friend who has come to help you," said Jahdu in his kindest voice. "And what is your name?"

"I'm Young Owl," said the owl. "I'm friendly with a lady barn owl who lives on the edge of this wood. Her name is Lilly. It's her birthday today and for two days I've tried to find a present for her. That's the reason I have a headache."

"Well, why don't you give her a weasel or two?" said Jahdu. He knew that owls were fond of weasels.

"That's just the problem," said Young Owl. "Lilly has everything. She has plenty of weasels and white mice, too. But she doesn't have any place to keep them."

"Woogily!" whispered Jahdu to himself. "I know how to catch me an owl!"

"What is it you say? I didn't hear you," said Young Owl.

"I said, I can help you for sure, Young Owl," said Jahdu. "I have just the thing for your lady owl. If you'll step outside I'll show it to you. It's a fine gift and a good place to keep weasels and mice."

"Ohhhh. Hooooo. No," said Young Owl, holding his tufts. "I can't go out with this headache, for the sun would blind me."

"Oh, for goodness sake," said Jahdu. "Keep your eyes closed and I will lead you. What I have for your lady owl is up the tree across from here. Come along now."

Young Owl let Jahdu take hold of his wing and lead him over to the tree where Jahdu had hung the parakeet cage.

Young Owl kept his eyes tight shut. "I hope you know what you're doing, friend," he said to Jahdu. "I've *never* walked up a tree."

"Don't worry," said Jahdu. "A few more steps and we'll be among the branches and leaves. You'll be able to open your eyes in the shade."

Soon Jahdu and Young Owl walked among the branches of the tree. But sunlight fell brightly through the leaves. In a moment Young Owl had reached a place right in front of Jahdu's parakeet cage.

"You may stop now," Jahdu told Young Owl. Jahdu reached around Young Owl to open the cage.

"Young Owl, open your eyes," said Jahdu.

44

Young Owl opened his eyes. When he saw the parakeet cage, he gave a loud screech. Yes, he did. Jahdu pushed Young Owl inside the cage and slammed the door shut.

"Woogily!" said Jahdu. "Jahdu has caught himself an owl!"

"Jahdu!" Young Owl said. "You, Jahdu! I've heard about you, who play tricks for fun. Oh, please, let me go. I hate sunlight. I hate cages!"

"I won't let you go, no indeed," said Jahdu. "I'm going to sit down beside you and sing happy songs to you until I am too tired to sing. I know about forty happy songs," Jahdu added, "and I never grow tired of singing!"

Jahdu sat himself down next to the cage. He had no one else to stop along with, so he had plenty of time. He sang at the top of his voice for the whole sun-filled day. Yes, he did.

Young Owl lay on his stomach on the floor of the cage. He moaned and groaned and held tightly onto the tufts on his head. Like most owls, he did not like anything bright or happy. He felt best being sad.

"Ohhhhh! Hooooo!" Young Owl cried. "I hate sunlight! I hate cages! I hate all happy songs!"

When the day was over, Jahdu jumped to the ground. He cleared his voice, for it had grown husky from singing happy songs. "Well, Young Owl," Jahdu called up the tree, "Jahdu has to be running along. I'm sure your lady friend will come as soon as it's dark. She'll want her present, of course, and you can give her your cage!"

Jahdu picked up the can of blue paint and placed it on his head.

Young Owl watched Jahdu. Even with a headache Young Owl was a curious sort.

"Would you mind telling me why you have that can of blue paint on your head?" Young Owl asked Jahdu.

"I don't mind at all," said Jahdu. "I'm carrying it, you dumb owl! I intend to paint somebody blue!"

So Jahdu went on his way with the can of blue paint on his head, and every now and then he would swing along on the vines as big as snakes. Jahdu had a good time swinging and running along through the wood in this new place. Jahdu hadn't yet found anybody he felt like painting blue. But he would find somebody soon. Yes, he would.

That is how Jahdu outwitted Young Owl. Jahdu had outwitted almost everybody by now. And almost everybody had grown very tired of Jahdu.

THIS IS THE END OF THE JAHDU STORY FILLED WITH MISCHIEF THAT MAMA LUKA TOLD TO THE CHILD, LEE EDWARD.

HOW JAHDU BECAME HIMSELF

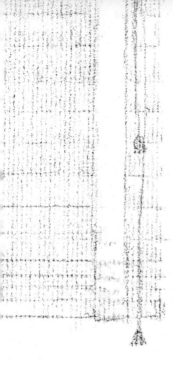

Summer had come to the good place called Harlem. The window was open wide in Mama Luka's hot little room. Mama Luka had moved her chair closer to the window. Yes, she had. She had raised her blind so that she could see what happened in the street below.

"Yes, child," she said to Lee Edward, who sat on the floor. "I have seen fifty summers come to that street down there and with each summer will come Jahdu just running along."

"Will I get to see him this summer?" asked Lee Edward.

"You might have a hard time seeing him, Little Brother," Mama Luka said. "Jahdu is never the same."

49

"Not even his face?" asked Lee Edward. He hoped this time to catch Mama Luka before she had time to think.

"Anyone who has seen the face of Jahdu will tell you *only* that it is never the same," said Mama Luka carefully. "But there is a steady light from his eyes," she said. "There is pride in his face that is always the same."

"I will look for Jahdu," said Lee Edward. "I will look for the pride in every face I see."

"You know, I start baking bread in the summertime," Mama Luka told Lee Edward. "I always think that maybe this time Jahdu will stop and visit with me and tell me what he has been up to."

"Has Jahdu ever stopped by to visit with you?" asked Lee Edward.

Mama Luka stared out her window. She spoke softly to Lee Edward. "I am baking bread right now," she said. "I am baking bread and I am hoping."

"I can smell the bread," Jahdu said. "It smells very good, too."

"Yes, child," said Mama Luka, turning from the window. "I never told you before, but Jahdu was born in an oven beside two loaves of baking bread." Mama Luka smiled. "One loaf baked brown and the other baked black. Jahdu didn't bake at all. But since that time black and brown have been Jahdu's favorite colors and the smell of baking bread is the sweetest smell to him."

Then Lee Edward pointed to the window sill all of a sudden. Mama Luka understood and she cupped her hands around the place Lee Edward had pointed to. Mama Luka opened her mouth and swallowed what had been in her hands.

"Oh, yes," she said. "Little Brother, that's the best old story you picked out of the air. It makes me feel cool and fresh inside."

"Then tell it," Lee Edward said to Mama Luka.

"I'm getting myself ready," said Mama Luka.

THIS IS THE JAHDU STORY SO COOL AND FRESH THAT MAMA LUKA TOLD TO LEE EDWARD.

Jahdu was running along. He was telling everybody to get out of his way. Everybody always did get out of Jahdu's way. Except this time somebody wouldn't and that somebody was Grass.

Grass lay on the ground in one dull shade of gray as far as the eye could see. Jahdu shouted at him. "Get out of the way, Grass, for Jahdu is coming through."

Grass didn't move at all. No, he didn't. Jahdu lay down on Grass and stretched himself out as far as he could.

"How do you like that, Uncle No-Color?" Jahdu said to Grass. "Jahdu is heavy, isn't he?"

Grass didn't say a word. But Grass couldn't feel the sunlight with Jahdu stretched out on him and he grew cold. And when Jahdu called him Uncle No-Color, he became very angry.

Grass lifted all his young gray blades straight as arrows. He pushed them against Jahdu with all his might. And the strain on his young gray blades turned each and every one of them green. To this day you can tell Grass whenever you chance to see him. For each and every one of his blades is still green.

Well, Jahdu laughed. He got up slowly. He yawned two or three times and gave no more thought to Grass, who had turned green.

Jahdu kept right on running along. He was running eastward, for he had been born in the East. And Jahdu had an idea he might like to be born again into something else. He ran and he ran until he came to dry, hot sand.

"Woogily!" Jahdu whispered. "This sand is hotter than anything I know that is hot."

Jahdu saw Ocean lying as calm as could be on the horizon where the hot sand ended.

Jahdu screamed in his meanest voice. "Hey, Uncle Calm Ocean! Why don't you once in a while get up and give the sand something to cool itself with? Lying around all day, watering the clouds and cooling off the birds. Why don't you get yourself together long enough to help out the hot sand?"

Old Ocean wasn't bad. But he was used to being the biggest somebody around under the sky. He was used to not moving, just lying there as cool and blue as he pleased. Ocean knew he was bigger and wetter and deeper than anything under the sun. And when Jahdu said what he had, all grew still. The wind stopped its blowing. Ocean himself stopped being lazy long enough to think about what Jahdu had said.

All at once Ocean gathered himself together right across his middle. He gave a heave that lifted his body higher than he had ever lifted it before. Ocean started moving from the horizon over the sand in a white, foaming line treetop tall.

"Woogily!" said Jahdu. And he went on running.

Old Ocean leaped right in front of Jahdu. But Ocean didn't catch Jahdu. For Jahdu surely knew how to keep running along. Every time Ocean slid back to the horizon to gather himself together again, Jahdu would run away somewhere else. Ocean would hit the hot sand with all his might only to find that Jahdu had run by.

To this day Ocean keeps on moving up and back and up and back again. He keeps on trying to catch anything passing by.

Jahdu kept right on running along. He was growing tired. He felt like stopping to rest. But he had no friend he could stop along with. He had played so many tricks nobody trusted him.

Mrs. Alligator used to give Jahdu free rides on her back. But not anymore, for Jahdu had come along one time with a can of blue paint on his head. He had put Mrs. Alligator to sleep and then he had painted her skin with two coats of blue paint. The paint hadn't worn off for a year. Now Mrs. Alligator thought Jahdu had manners worse than a crocodile's. Whenever she heard Jahdu running along, she would dive deep to the bottom of her pool. Yes, she would.

Jahdu came alongside a shade tree. The shade tree had leaves as big as elephant's ears. It had a trunk smooth to lean against. So Jahdu sat himself down. He leaned against the tree trunk and rested. He let the leaves as big as elephant's ears fan him. Jahdu soon felt like taking a nap. He was almost asleep when he heard a voice next to him.

"Stranger, kindly move off my tail!" said the voice. "Hey, you, sir, who will lean against a body without a pardon me!"

"Woogily!" said Jahdu, and he jumped five feet away from the tree.

It wasn't the shade tree who had spoken. Shade trees do not speak and do not care who leans against them. It was old Chameleon who had spoken. Chameleon was a lizard six inches long. He had not seen Jahdu for many a month. But when Jahdu said "Woogily!" Chameleon knew him right away.

"Jahdu," Chameleon said, "I wish you would learn to ask somebody when you want to lean on somebody."

Jahdu looked all around. It took him a minute to see the lizard on the tree trunk. Jahdu had always liked Chameleon. Chameleon could change the color of his skin any time he felt like it. If Chameleon sat down on a green leaf, he would turn himself green and nobody could tell he was sitting on the leaf. If he wanted to sit on a flat stone, he would turn himself the color of the flat stone. And nobody need know he was resting awhile.

At last Jahdu saw Chameleon on the trunk of the shade tree. Chameleon was brown as was the dark brown tree trunk.

"Well, how are you doing?" Jahdu said, coming closer.

"You stay right where you are!" shouted Chameleon. "Don't come any nearer until you promise you won't tie my tail in a knot."

"Oh, my goodness," Jahdu said, sitting down.

"I mean what I say," Chameleon told Jahdu. "The last time you tied my tail up I had an awful time getting it untied."

"How *did* you get it untied?" Jahdu wanted to know. He spoke to the lizard in his kindest voice. For Jahdu knew now that he wanted something special from the lizard.

"Never you mind how I got myself loose," said Chameleon. "You just promise."

So Jahdu promised. Then he and the lizard sat against the trunk of the shade tree.

"I've just been running along," Jahdu told his friend Chameleon.

"All right," said Chameleon.

"I had a little fun with Grass," said Jahdu.

"That's good," said the lizard. "Grass is always so gray and sad."

"Not anymore," Jahdu said. "Grass is now green as he can be!"

"All right," Chameleon said. "Green is brighter than gray."

"I had a little fun with Ocean," Jahdu told his friend.

"That's all right," said Chameleon. "Ocean always did lie too far back on the horizon."

"Not anymore," Jahdu told him. "Now Ocean rises treetop tall. He runs over the hot sand hilltop high and then he falls down trying to catch anything running along."

"That's good, too," said the lizard. "Now the hot sand will get a chance to cool itself."

"So I have stopped awhile from running along," said Jahdu.

"All right," Chameleon said.

"I have stopped and now I know why I was running along and what I want from you," said Jahdu.

"Tell me then," said the lizard.

"I want to know how you work your magic," said Jahdu.

"You already have your own magic," Chameleon told Jahdu. "You can put anything to sleep and wake anything up again."

"But I need to know the magic you have," said Jahdu to his friend.

"What magic is that?" Chameleon asked Jahdu.

"You can change to look like a stone or even a leaf," Jahdu told him.

"Sure, I can," said the lizard, "but I can't let you do that, too."

"Well, I know you can't my friend," Jahdu said. "I only want to know how you do it. If I know how it is you can change and hide, maybe I can learn how to just change into something else."

"Change into what?" Chameleon wanted to know.

"Change myself into whatever I want," Jahdu told him. "If I see a deer, I can be a deer running through the woods. If I see a fox, I can be as swift and clever as a fox."

Chameleon smiled. "It's not hard," he told Jahdu. "I will tell you what I do. With a bit of practice maybe it will work for you."

"Tell me then," said Jahdu.

"First I see a place where I want to sit," Chameleon said. "Then I think about what it feels like sitting there. Next I run as fast as I can to get there. And then I sit. And the color of the thing I'm sitting on comes over me right away."

"That's all you do?" Jahdu asked. "Woogily!" he said. "Changing is going to be easy!"

Suddenly Jahdu looked unhappy. "How am I going to run fast enough to catch up with a deer and climb on his back?" he asked the lizard.

"Maybe you won't have to run at all," said Chameleon. "Maybe you will only need to see the deer running fast."

"Then what?" Jahdu asked.

"Then you think hard," said Chameleon. "You say to yourself, 'Jahdu is running as fast as that deer. Jahdu is on that deer. Jahdu *is* that deer!'"

"Woogily!" said Jahdu.

"Try it," Chameleon told Jahdu.

Jahdu left his friend Chameleon dozing against the trunk of the shade tree. Jahdu went running along. He had not seen anything yet that he wanted to be. He was still running eastward to where he had been born.

"The first thing I see that I like, I will be," Jahdu said to himself. And he kept right on running along.

Jahdu came to an island. The island had buildings higher than high. Jahdu liked the buildings. Yes, he did.

He said, "Woogily!" and kept on running. "I'm going to make myself into a building."

Jahdu picked out for himself a building higher than a hilltop. He thought very hard. "Jahdu is running to that building," he said to himself. "Jahdu is on top of that building. Jahdu *is* that building!"

Jahdu became a building made of steel and concrete. He was very tall, but he could not move. Jahdu did not like standing still.

"Woogily!" said Jahdu. He thought very quickly and he said to himself, "Jahdu is jumping off this building. Jahdu is running away from this building. Jahdu is not a building anymore!"

Jahdu kept right on running along. He ran and he ran through the city on an island. He saw a stray cat and he became the cat. But Jahdu didn't like being a cat. He was always hungry. He was sick and he was tired and he slept where he could. Jahdu was thrown out of a supermarket for trying to get at the frozen fish.

"Woogily!" said Jahdu. "Cats have a hard time getting along. Jahdu is jumping off this cat. Jahdu is running faster than this cat. Jahdu is not a cat anymore!"

Jahdu kept on running. He saw an orange-and-black taxicab.

"Woogily!" said Jahdu. "I'm going to be that taxicab." And so he was.

Now Jahdu was busy taking people from one place to another. But he didn't much like being a taxicab. People sat down too hard on his seats and tracked dirt in on his floor. People were afraid when he went very fast. Jahdu worked for long hours. Yes, he did. And the bright lights of the city hurt his eyes.

"Jahdu is jumping off this taxicab," Jahdu said at the end of a long day. "Jahdu is moving faster than that pretty orange-and-black taxicab. Jahdu is not a taxicab anymore!"

The taxicab drove away. Jahdu kept right on running along. He found himself in a fine, good place called Harlem. Yes, he did.

"Woogily!" said Jahdu. "All the people here are brown and black."

Jahdu came upon a group of children playing in a playground. He saw a small, black boy who was running around making noise.

"Woogily!" said Jahdu. "Jahdu is running as fast as that black child. Jahdu is jumping on that black child. Jahdu *is* that black child!"

Black was Jahdu's favorite color and Jahdu was now a strong, black child. He didn't own a baseball or a bat. But he had a dog. Yes, Jahdu did. And the dog's name was Rufus. And the dog was black all over, just like Jahdu. Jahdu had a sister and a brother too. And Jahdu had a good time in the city on the island.

Jahdu was happy. He was a strong, black boy. For a while he stayed in the neighborhood, just enjoying himself.

THIS IS THE END OF THE JAHDU STORY SO COOL AND FRESH THAT MAMA LUKA TOLD TO THE CHILD, LEE EDWARD.

"You picked the story," Mama Luka said. "It was a good story and Jahdu was happy being a strong, black boy."

"The way I am happy?" asked Lee Edward.

"Just the way you are happy," said Mama Luka.

"Did the strong, black boy have the Jahdu magic?" asked Lee Edward.

"The strong, black boy was still a small, black boy," said Mama Luka. "And, Little Brother, a small, black boy doesn't have too much magic, even when he's Jahdu. He could put his mama to sleep by making her read him one storybook after another. And he could wake his papa up fast enough by saying he had been a building once upon a time. But he didn't have much more magic than that."

"I don't see how Jahdu of all the Jahdu stories could like being a small, black child," said Lee Edward. "I would think he'd rather be a building."

"You think about it for awhile," Mama Luka told Lee Edward. "I'll take myself a little nap for five or six minutes." Mama Luka always did like sleeping after telling a good Jahdu story.

Mama Luka went right to sleep in her chair and sitting on her long black braid. The smell of baking bread was strong and sweet in the room.

61

Lee Edward went to Mama Luka's kitchen not much bigger than a closet on one side of the room. He peeked into the oven. The large loaf of bread he found had baked brown and was done. Lee Edward took the loaf of bread out of the oven and placed it on the counter. He turned off the oven and stood sniffing the bread that smelled sweeter than anything. And then Lee Edward lay on his back on the floor beside Mama Luka's chair and thought about Jahdu.

Pretty soon Lee Edward closed his eyes and smiled. A little later he opened his eyes and laughed. He knew why Jahdu was happy being a strong, black boy.

Lee Edward imagined Jahdu's changing from a strong, black boy into a bigger, stronger boy. As Jahdu grew, he had more and more magic power. Something Mama Luka had said about Jahdu came to him.

"There is pride in his face that is always the same."

Little Brother had to smile.

"Once he's grown up he'll be a black Jahdu with all his power," whispered Lee Edward.

He pointed to a space of air close to Mama Luka's right foot. He thought he felt himself growing.

"I can have the pride and the power, too," Lee Edward said, and he waited for Mama Luka to wake up.

VIRGINIA HAMILTON was born in Yellow Springs, Ohio, a small town not unlike the Crystal of *Zeely*, her first book for children. After ten years in New York City, she has recently returned with her husband and two children to Yellow Springs to live.

She is particularly proud and conscious of her heritage, and attributes these feelings to her Ohio birthplace. Her grandfather Perry was one of the many thousands of slaves who escaped from the South to Ohio, and she grew up in what had been one of the strongest stations of the Underground Railroad. The tradition and background of her childhood play an important role in the author's *The House of Dies Drear* and in all of her writing.

Both *Zeely* and *The House of Dies Drear* were chosen American Library Association Notable Books, and the enthusiastic reception accorded them has established Miss Hamilton as one of our leading writers for young people.

Miss Hamilton attended Antioch College and Ohio State University. As a hobby, she played the guitar and sang semiprofessionally, but she has wanted to be a writer as far back as she can remember.

NONNY HOGROGIAN, a native New Yorker, is a graduate of Hunter College and attended the Haystack Mountain School of Crafts in Maine.

Even her earliest art efforts were appreciated. Her father's avocation is painting and as a small girl Nonny would "improve" on some of his brush strokes with her own. Her talent was immediately evident and papa thoroughly enjoyed his young daughter's embellishments.

Miss Hogrogian's career started as a children's book designer, but she very soon began to illustrate books as well. Her success was rapid, and in 1966 she won the Caldecott Medal, given for "the most distinguished picture book for children," for *Always Room for One More* by Sorche Nic Leodhas.

Miss Hogrogian now designs only her own books and devotes her full time to illustrating.